18088

||||||||||||||||||||||||||||||||

W9-CME-238

DATE DUE

JUL 13 1995	NOV 7 '98	JUN 0 2 2008	
AUG. 1 4 1995	NOV 21 '98	AUG 0 2 2008	
NOV. 2 4 1995	NOV 27 '99		
JUL. 1 1 1996	JUL 2 7 1999	APR 1 8 2011	
JUL. 2 3 1996		JUL 2 7 2011	
AUG 29 1997	JUL 0 4 2001		
SEP 0 6 1997	MAR 1 8 2002		
SEP 2 7 199	JUN 2 7 2002		
OCT 22 '98	JUL 0 5 2002		
NOV 3 '98	JUL 2 4 2003		
	JUL 1 0 2006		

E
Dod   Dodds, Siobhan
Grandpa Bud

THIS CANDLEWICK BOOK BELONGS TO:

For Nana and Grandad

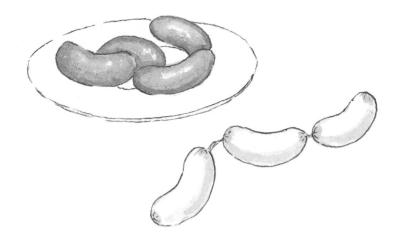

Copyright © 1993 by Siobhan Dodds

First U.S. paperback edition 1995

Library of Congress Cataloging-in-Publication Data

Dodds, Siobhan.
Grandpa Bud / Siobhan Dodds.—1st U.S. ed.
Summary: A grandfather busily prepares all kinds of food for
his granddaughter and the guests he thinks she is bringing to visit him.
[1. Grandfathers—Fiction. 2. Toys—Fiction.] I. Title.
PZ7.D6629Gr 1993   92-53135
[E]—dc20
ISBN 1-56402-175-0(hardcover)—ISBN 1-56402-489-X(paperback).

2 4 6 8 10 9 7 5 3 1

Printed in Hong Kong

The pictures in this book were done in
watercolor and pen and ink.

Candlewick Press
2067 Massachusetts Avenue
Cambridge, Massachusetts 02140

Grandpa Bud
Siobhan Dodds

CANDLEWICK PRESS
CAMBRIDGE, MASSACHUSETTS

"Hello, Grandpa Bud.
Mommy said I could
come over and stay
the night and if I'm
good you might make
me a chocolate cake.
Chocolate cake is
my favorite food.
Don't worry, Grandpa Bud—
I won't be any trouble."

What a surprise for Grandpa Bud!
Polly is coming to stay.

Quick, quick, quick!
A chocolate cake for Polly.

ring
ring
ring

"Hello, Grandpa Bud. Can Henry come too? He won't be any trouble. Henry has a big Band-Aid on his knee. He was doing cartwheels in the yard and he fell over. He didn't cry. He told me that Jell-O and ice cream will make his knee better. Don't worry, Grandpa Bud. Henry can sleep in my bed."

What a surprise for Grandpa Bud! Henry is coming to stay.

Quick, quick, quick!
Jell-O and ice cream for Henry.
Oh, and a chocolate cake
for Polly!

ring
ring
ring

"Hello, Grandpa Bud.
Can Rosie come too?
She won't be any trouble.
Rosie isn't feeling very
good today. I think she
has a cold. She sneezed four
times this morning. She likes
banana sandwiches best. Don't worry,
Grandpa Bud. Rosie can
sleep in my bed too."

What a surprise for
Grandpa Bud! Rosie
is coming
to stay.

Quick, quick, quick!
Banana sandwiches for Rosie.
Jell-O and ice cream for Henry.
Oh, and a chocolate cake
for Polly!

ring
ring
ring

"Hello, Grandpa Bud.
Can George come too?
He won't be any trouble.
George has red polka-dot
shorts and a big, fat tummy.
His favorite food is hot dogs.
Don't worry, Grandpa Bud.
George can sleep in
my bed too."

What a surprise
for Grandpa Bud!
George is
coming
to stay.

Quick, quick, quick!
Hot dogs for George.
Banana sandwiches for Rosie.
Jell-O and ice cream for Henry.
Oh, and a chocolate cake
for Polly!

Knock
Knock
Knock

"Hello, Grandpa Bud.
This is Henry,
this is Rosie,
and this is George."

What a surprise
for Grandpa Bud!
Oh, and...

...what an enormous feast for Polly!

"Good night, Grandpa Bud.
It's lots of fun coming to stay."

SIOBHAN DODDS says the telephone was the ideal vehicle for this story "because of the obvious fascination young children have with phones and because a phone's *ring-ring-ring* works well when read aloud." Siobhan Dodds is also the author-illustrator of *Words and Pictures*.